SHORT TALES

Fables

The Town Mouse and the Country Mouse

Adapted by Christopher E. Long
Illustrated by Mark Bloodworth

magic wagon

visit us at www.abdopublishing.com

Published by Magic Wagon, a division of the ABDO Group, 8000 West 78th Street, Edina, Minnesota, 55439. Copyright © 2010 by Abdo Consulting Group, Inc. International copyrights reserved in all countries. All rights reserved. No part of this book may be reproduced in any form without written permission from the publisher.

Short Tales ™ is a trademark and logo of Magic Wagon.

Printed in the United States of America, North Mankato, Minnesota.
092009
012010

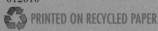 PRINTED ON RECYCLED PAPER

Adapted Text by Christopher E. Long
Illustrations by Mark Bloodworth
Colors by Hi-Fi
Edited by Stephanie Hedlund and Rochelle Baltzer
Interior Layout by Kristen Fitzner Denton
Book Design and Packaging by Shannon Eric Denton

Library of Congress Cataloging-in-Publication Data

Long, Christopher E.
   The town mouse and the country mouse / adapted by Christopher E. Long ; illustrated by Mark Bloodworth.
      p. cm. -- (Short tales. Fables)
   ISBN 978-1-60270-556-2
   [1. Fables. 2. Folklore.] I. Bloodworth, Mark, ill. II. Aesop. III. Title.
   PZ8.2.L65To 2010
   398.2--dc22
   [E]
                            2008032324

One day, Town Mouse went to visit his cousin.

Country Mouse welcomed Town Mouse into his home.

"Your home is small," Town Mouse said.

"But it's warm and peaceful," Country Mouse said.

Country Mouse served Town Mouse dinner.

"Everything is much better in town,"
Town Mouse said.

"Come with me and I'll show you how to live," Town Mouse said.

"Your home is very large," Country Mouse said.

"Yes, I am," said Country Mouse.

"This is what we eat in town," Town Mouse said.

Suddenly, the cousins heard barking.

They had to run and hide.

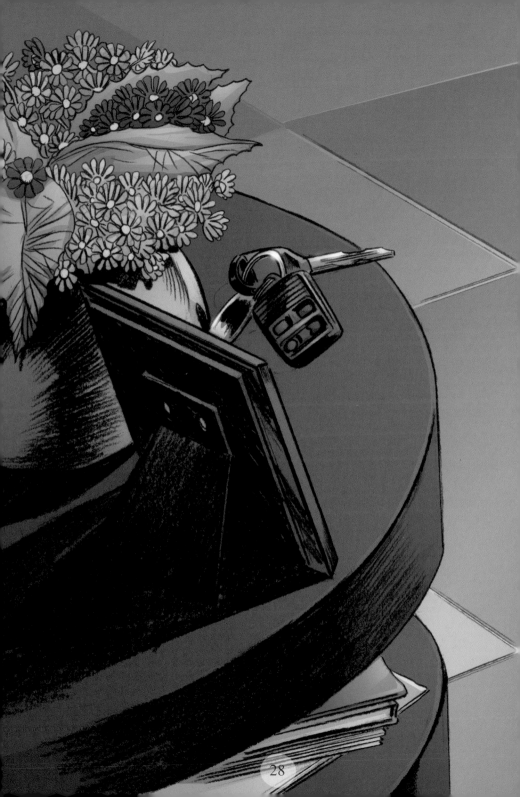

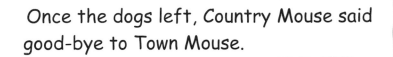

Once the dogs left, Country Mouse said good-bye to Town Mouse.

"Better beans and bacon in peace than cakes in fear," he said.

The moral of the story is:

Better a little in safety, than much surrounded by danger.